Sa and the Boots

Written by Jill Eggleton
Illustrated by Jim Storey

The sailors were cleaning the deck. They were not happy.

Sailor Sam looked at them.
"I will make you laugh,"
he said.

"You can't make us laugh,"
said the sailors.

Sailor Sam sat in a bucket.
The sailors did not laugh.

Sailor Sam put the bucket on his head.
The sailors did not laugh.

Sailor Sam saw
the captain.
She was asleep in the chair.
"I will take her boots,"
said Sailor Sam.

Sailor Sam got the boots.

He went up the mast.

The captain woke up.
"Where are my boots?"
she shouted.
"They are not on my feet."

She looked under the chair.

She looked under the ropes.

"Did you take my boots?"
she said.

The captain looked up.
Sailor Sam was
in the sails.

The captain
did not see Sailor Sam.
But she saw a bird.
"Look," she said.
"That bird had my boots."

The sailors laughed and laughed.

"It's not funny," said the captain. "You can't take off your boots on this boat."

A Comic Strip

Guide Notes

Title: Sailor Sam and the Boots
Stage: Early (3) – Blue

Genre: Fiction
Approach: Guided Reading
Processes: Thinking Critically, Exploring Language, Processing Information
Written and Visual Focus: Comic Strip, Speech Bubbles

THINKING CRITICALLY
(sample questions)
- What do you think this story could be about? Look at the title and discuss.
- Look at the cover. Why do you think Sailor Sam is sneaking around the deck?
- Look at pages 2 and 3. Why do you think the sailors weren't happy?
- Look at pages 4 and 5. What else do you think Sailor Sam could do to make the sailors laugh?
- Look at pages 6 and 7. Why do you think the captain has boots, but the sailors do not?
- Look at pages 10 and 11. Look at the captain pointing at the sailors. How do you think they feel? What do you think the sailors could say to the captain?
- Look at pages 12 and 13. Why do you think Sailor Sam is hiding?

EXPLORING LANGUAGE

Terminology
Title, cover, illustrations, author, illustrator

Vocabulary
Interest words: sailors, bucket, mast, captain, laugh, deck
High-frequency words: did, take, that, them, there, were, off
Positional words: in, on, up, under, off

Print Conventions
Capital letter for sentence beginnings and names (**S**ailor **S**am), periods, commas, exclamation mark, quotation marks, question marks